nickel

Trouble with Trix

The Junior Novelization

randomhouse.com/kids

ISBN: 978-0-307-97995-7

Printed in the United States of America

10 9 8 7 6 5 4 3 2 1

NICKELODEON

WINX CLUB

Trouble with Trix

The Junior Novelization

Adapted by Randi Reisfeld

Random House 🏠 New York

Chapter 1

It was a beautiful morning in the Magic Dimension. A teenage girl named Bloom and her four fairy friends were on their way to school. They were in their second month of classes at Alfea College for Fairies, the best school for fairies-in-training. Bloom's friends and roommates—golden-haired Stella, musically gifted Musa, nature-loving Flora, and technologically talented Tecna—had known they were fairies from birth. But Bloom had only recently discovered she had special powers.

As Bloom and her friends walked across the school's courtyard, Stella was telling about the story of how she had met Bloom.

"I was in the middle of a battle with a bloodthirsty ogre and his horrific ghouls, and even though I *am* Stella, Fairy of the Shining Sun, even *I* feel outnumbered sometimes." Stella grimaced. "I was about to be defeated when all of a sudden, this red-haired girl with a cute pet bunny burst into the picture. She yelled for the ghouls to back off, and magic shot from her fingers, and the whole lot of them got zapped into a million pieces!"

Flora groaned. "You've told this story a million times, Stella."

"But it's still exciting, isn't it?" Stella tossed her blond hair over her shoulder. "Anyway, if it weren't for me, Bloom would have never unlocked her fairy powers. Once I found out she was magical, I knew she had to come to Alfea College right away to begin her training as a fairy. If I hadn't been on Earth that one day, Bloom would have spent her life as an ordinary human, never knowing she had the super-strong power of the Dragon Flame inside her!" Stella sighed happily. "You have a lot to thank me for, don't you, Bloom?" She paused. "Bloom? Bloom?"

There was no answer. Bloom had a troubled expression on her face. She seemed lost in thought.

"What's wrong?" asked Stella.

"I had another strange dream last night," Bloom confessed.

"Was it scary?" asked Musa.

"No, it wasn't a nightmare," Bloom said, "but I can't stop thinking about it."

"More details," Tecna said. The fairy with the short, choppy magenta hair was the most logical of Bloom's new friends. She used futuristic gadgets that hadn't been invented on Earth yet, some of which she had created herself. Tecna reached into her pocket and flipped open a round, palm-sized "dream probe" to interpret Bloom's dream.

"It's hard to explain." Bloom ran a hand through her thick, fiery-red hair. "But it felt a lot more vivid than a dream!"

"Mmm-hmm, go on," Tecna coaxed.

"There was a woman. She was calling to me." As Bloom recalled the story of her dream, her mind was swept back into it. She had been flying through complete darkness, but she knew she was heading toward something, or some*one*—a willowy-voiced woman who kept calling to her.

"Bloom, we meet again, my little one!" the woman had said.

"Yes, I hear you!" Bloom had called back. It was always the same sweet, melodious voice, but in her earlier dreams, Bloom hadn't seen the woman's face.

This time, she saw it—partly, at least. A vision of a glowing, beautiful face had appeared out of the darkness. The woman had long, flowing blond hair that reached out to Bloom like octopus tentacles. She wore an orange and gold mask that covered her eyes. Even so, something about her was familiar.

"Where am I?" Bloom had asked the vision. "This isn't Alfea College!"

"I know," responded the woman. "And we don't have much time!"

"Time? For what? Who are you?"

"I am Daphne. Listen carefully, Bloom!" The woman sounded desperate.

Daphne. Where had Bloom heard that name before?

"You must come to me!" Daphne had insisted.

"But why?" Bloom asked.

Bloom didn't get an answer, only more pleas. "Yes, Bloom, come to me! You must come to me!" Daphne's voice was weakening.

"Here I am!" Bloom called, reaching toward the shimmering figure. "I'm coming!"

Then, in a blinding flash of light, Daphne disappeared.

"Daphneeee!" Bloom had called in her sleep. "I'm coming, Daphne!" With a start, Bloom had awakened in a cold sweat. The dream had been so vivid that for a moment, she had frantically searched around her room, expecting Daphne to be hovering somewhere.

Bloom took a deep breath and shivered. "Do you have any idea what it means?" she asked Tecna.

Tecna peered at the dream probe. A ladybug emerged from the probe's core and fluttered around Bloom's head. Then it returned to its nest inside the probe. Tecna announced, "There is a strong possibility that the dream was a psycho-magic message."

"Are you saying that she—Daphne—was trying to communicate with me?"

Tecna nodded. "Through your dream. Yes." She held up the dream probe and explained. "From the memory waves she left in your brain, I came up with this." A hologram projected the face of a masked blond woman. "What do you think? Is this her?"

"It is!" Bloom gasped. "It's Daphne!" How had Tecna done that? It was mind-boggling! Then Bloom suddenly remembered something. "I've seen her somewhere else, outside my dreams—"

A memory—a real one—popped up in Bloom's brain. "Of course! Now I remember!"

A few days before, Bloom and her friends had taken a trip to Magix, the big city outside Alfea. "It happened in the main square in Magix," Bloom told Tecna. "That's where I saw her."

The city was crowded that day. Hundreds of people were rushing along the narrow sidewalks in the shadows cast by the tall buildings.

"But," Bloom continued as the memory sharpened, "Daphne wasn't in the crowds. She was *on* something."

Bloom thought back. At one point, she'd gazed skyward, admiring the skyscrapers. That was where she'd seen Daphne! Her image, along with other beautiful, dreamlike faces, was carved on the side of one of the buildings. Bloom even recalled the words imprinted under the picture: THE NYMPHS OF MAGIX.

The nymph carved in the center had been bigger than all the others. She wore a mask that Bloom recognized. It was Daphne!

"I remember her because she was looking right at me," Bloom blurted out. She peered up at her friends and blushed. "Sorry, guys. I feel a little silly. After all, I'm talking about a carving as if it were alive."

"She's real!" Stella said, jumping in. "If Daphne's face was put on the side of a building, she's probably famous. I'm willing to bet she was super-powerful."

Bloom considered this. Stella did seem to be making sense. In big cities on Earth, super-famous people were often pictured on billboards. "So if Daphne was famous here in the Magic Dimension . . . ," she began.

"We can look her up in the library!" Stella finished.

Chapter 2

The next day before class, Bloom headed to the library to find information on Daphne. The other Winx were busy, so Bloom brought Kiko along instead. The pet bunny was more than happy to hop along with Bloom and discover new places.

As she walked through the corridors of the college, Bloom thought about how important books were in her life. She loved them. Not too long before, books had been her only source of information about fairies. Bloom was obsessed with magical beings and read everything she could about them. Her parents had thought she would outgrow her fascination. They didn't understand what Bloom had felt all her life. As crazy as it sounded to say out loud, deep down, she'd believed she really was a fairy. She just couldn't prove it. Or do anything about it.

Then came the day she met Stella. Bloom had been at the park with Kiko. The little gray-and-white bunny had hopped away to explore but had returned only minutes later, frightened out of his wits. Bloom had gone to investigate. Deep in the forested section of the park, in an isolated clearing, a girl with long blond hair and glittering wings was trying to defend herself against a giant ogre.

The ogre was ugly, mean, and had help: a pack of frightening ghouls!

Drawn into the battle, Bloom was somehow able to shield the girl and scare off the creatures. It was . . . magical.

That was when Stella had introduced herself and figured that Bloom, too, must be a fairy. Bloom would never forget Stella's words: "If you throw up energy shields like a fairy and beat down monsters like a fairy, you must be a fairy!"

Shortly after Stella had declared that Bloom was a fairy, the ogre, the ghouls, and a hideous blue-skinned troll attacked Bloom's house. Bloom and Stella battled the evil gang using their magical fairy powers, but they were outnumbered.

In the nick of time, four guys called the Specialists showed up to help out. They were wizards-in-training at Redfountain, the school right next to Alfea College. There was dark-haired Brandon; Timmy, the tech master of the group; purple-haired Riven, who had some serious attitude; and charming, blue-eyed Prince Sky. Working together, the Specialists, Stella, and Bloom had defeated the monsters.

The rest had happened so quickly. Stella had convinced Bloom's parents to allow their daughter to attend Alfea College, and Stella had brought her to Magix. In the short time she'd been there, Bloom had formed tight friendships with her roommates, Tecna, Stella, Musa, and Flora. They'd decided to call themselves the Winx Club, and had already experienced several exciting adventures.

Bloom thought back to her last adventure with the Winx. They had been completely alone in Alfea, challenged by the grumpy assistant headmistress, Griselda, to clean the school without using their magic, while the rest of the students were away on a field trip. Facing such an enormous task, the Winx had to think fast. They invited the Specialists over to help and had successfully finished the job, when a Minotaur had come tearing through the halls of the college.

The Minotaur had been unleashed by a trio of devious witches from a nearby school called Cloudtower. The witches, who called themselves the Trix, were searching for a powerful source of magical energy. Bloom, her friends, and the Specialists had been able to stop the Trix and the Minotaur without using magic, and the incident had brought the Winx and the Specialists closer together.

As she approached the entrance to the library, Bloom found herself daydreaming about her favorite Specialist, Prince Sky. He had been so brave fighting the Minotaur. Not to mention he had the most piercing blue eyes and the dreamiest smile. . . .

"Stop," Bloom scolded herself. There was research to be done. She had to find out about Daphne, the nymph who haunted her dreams. With a sigh she pushed open the library door and went inside.

Alfea's library was located in the center of the college's main castle building. Although she'd been in school for two months, Bloom had never visited the library. In fact, until the day before, she hadn't even known that Alfea *had* a library! As she gazed around, she was impressed. Rows of bookcases arranged in a semicircle extended as far as the eye could see. They faced a winged book stand that stood on a raised platform.

Bloom realized that she was stumped about how to even start searching for information about Daphne. Something about the setup made her think she wasn't supposed to look through the bookshelves. The winged book stand looked like a pedestal where she could use her magic to conjure up the book she wanted. Only . . . how would she get the book stand to work? Was it like GPS or a cell phone with voice recognition? Should she just say the word "Daphne" and expect a book with exactly the information she needed to magically appear? It was worth a try, especially since there seemed to be no one around besides her and Kiko. Bloom climbed onto the platform and placed her palms on a book rest in the center of the stand. She nervously cleared her throat and said, "Daphne!"

A fraction of a second later, a book flew off a shelf and plopped onto the stand. Bloom breathed a sigh of relief. She had guessed how to use the library correctly!

"Wow, that was really quick! Much faster than the Internet!" Bloom said. Magical libraries were awesome!

It got even better. The book opened by itself to a page labeled DAPHNE, and Bloom began to read. Then she frowned—she'd found a *definition* of the word. "No, I don't want to know what Daphne means.

I want to know about a fairy named Daphne!"

Bloom realized she needed to be more specific. She tried again. "Daphne the fairy!" she said firmly and clearly.

This time, two giant books flew out and opened to sections about Daphne the fairy. Bloom peered down at the pages. It seemed as though Daphne had been one of the most powerful Nymphs of Magix. She was the supreme fairy who had ruled over the Magic Dimension during the eons following the disappearance of the dragons.

Bloom scrunched her forehead. What did that mean? What eons? What dragons? And what did that have to do with the Daphne who was reaching out to her in her dreams? Bloom decided that to find out more, she needed to be even more specific. This time, palms down, she called out, "Daphne! A Nymph of Magix!"

Bloom looked up quickly, but not quickly enough to dodge the dozens of books that had flown off the shelves. Suspended in midair, they formed a circle around her. "Whoa, wait a minute!" Bloom shielded herself to prevent the books from getting too close and hitting her in the head. As if an invisible hand had switched on a supermixer, the airborne books began to whirl around her, faster and faster.

"Help!" Bloom cried out. "Enough books already!" Before she knew it, she was crouched on the floor, in the middle of a spinning cyclone of books, helpless to make it stop.

Luckily, someone else could.

"Closus!" a voice commanded. It was Miss Faragonda, headmistress of Alfea. The books stopped instantly and crashed to the floor. Trembling, a grateful Bloom hugged the headmistress.

"I'd say the library's research system needs a complete overhaul." Headmistress Faragonda sniffed, and then turned to the distraught Bloom. "It's all right; it's over now. Are you okay?"

"I think so," Bloom said shakily.

"Great. You can go, then." The headmistress dismissed Bloom abruptly with a wave of her hand.

Normally, Miss Faragonda was kind and helpful, but her tense face made it clear that she wasn't going to help Bloom find whatever she was searching for. "You can do your research another time," Miss Faragonda said, and turned away.

"Thank you," Bloom replied politely, and left the library. As she headed to class, she couldn't help being confused. Why had researching Daphne, a Nymph of Magix, stirred up a frenzy of books? Why had Miss Faragonda dismissed her so sharply? Something felt terribly wrong.

Bloom was right. As soon as the young fairy-in-training was out of sight, the headmistress looked through the books that had nearly attacked Bloom. She quickly summoned the chief librarian. "Miss Barbatea!"

"Yes?" A timid, bespectacled librarian scurried over.

"Put the books back in the stacks," Headmistress Faragonda directed, "and close the library."

"Yes, yes, of course," Miss Barbatea agreed—then stopped when she realized what she'd been told to do. "Huh? Close the library?"

"Yes," Miss Faragonda repeated, "and don't use magic."

The hapless librarian didn't question her boss, but she was having trouble understanding why the headmistress would want to close down the entire library.

"We must be very careful with Daphne. And Bloom," Miss Faragonda whispered. She took her job protecting the young fairy students very seriously. The less Bloom knew about Daphne, the safer she would be.

At that very moment, someone else was talking about Bloom and her friends—someone who did not have the fairies' best interests at heart. Down in Magix City, two people sat opposite each other in a small café. One was Darcy, a witch with pea-green hair and cat eyes. She belonged to the Trix, along with two other witches, Icy and Stormy. After Bloom had prevented the Trix from finding a powerful source of energy in Alfea, the Trix became sworn enemies of the Winx.

The person sitting opposite Darcy was Riven, one of the four Specialists who sided with the Winx. Riven, with his purple hair and perpetual sneer, was the most arrogant of the Specialists. He perched his elbows on the table, his T-shirt sleeves rolled up to display his ripped biceps and forearms.

After meeting Riven during a run-in with the Winx at Alfea, Darcy and the other members of the Trix had calculated that he might turn against the fairies—if the witches played their cards right. With that in mind, Darcy had invited Riven to a special meeting, and Riven, curious about what a witch wanted to say to him, had agreed to see her.

"I've been thinking about you, Riven," Darcy said conspiratorially. "Your talent . . . your ambition . . . your courage . . . are wasted with the Specialists." She pushed her hair from her face, revealing her stunning green eyes, which drew Riven in. "I know you want more. My sisters and I can make you powerful!"

"Go on," Riven said coolly. His voice sounded smooth and bored, but his eyes glittered with interest.

"We just need to know that you want to be with us, and that we can count on you." Darcy lowered her voice. With a wicked gleam in her eyes, she said, "Tell us all about those stinking little fairies, and we'll make you more powerful than you can possibly imagine."

Darcy reached across the table, and Riven intertwined his fingers with hers. The boy didn't say a word. But his eyes spoke volumes.

CHAPTER 3

The next Saturday was the beginning of school break. In the morning, Bloom awoke to the hustle and bustle of all the other fairy students getting ready to head home to their families. Everyone was excited and happy, except for Bloom, who was still troubled by her dreams. Bloom got out of bed groggily and found Flora zippering a suitcase.

"You're already packed?" Pajama-clad Bloom was surprised. She hadn't realized that her friends and roommates would be leaving immediately after breakfast.

"I can't wait to get home and see my family," Flora said. "Alfea is great, but I really miss my mom and dad." She laughed as Bloom rubbed her eyes. "C'mon, sleepyhead, get dressed!"

Bloom hurriedly slipped into her clothes and followed Flora into the common area they shared with Tecna, Stella, and Musa.

"Morning, sunshine!" Stella lounged on a comfy sofa, surrounded by six enormous suitcases.

"Whoa, Stella, we're only going to be gone for a week! Are you sure you want to bring all this luggage with you?" Bloom asked, raising her eyebrows.

Stella smiled. "Well, of course! After all, a fairy must be prepared for all situations—especially fashionable ones!"

Musa smiled shyly. "I just can't wait to go home and spend time with my parents. They're really great."

"I feel like I've been gone forever!" Flora admitted.

Tecna lifted her head from packing her own belongings. "Although your statement is emotional, I agree."

"Me too!" Bloom added, though not as quickly as Tecna and Flora. She was eager to return home, but

Alfea was so exciting, and she still had the mystery of Daphne and her strange dreams on her mind.

Half an hour later, Stella and Musa stood at their bedroom doors. "See you guys back here in a week!" Musa said, and gave each of the Winx a hug.

"I'm going to miss you guys." Bloom fought a catch in her throat.

"Oh, Bloom. We'll be back before you know it. Have a great vacation!" Stella said, and waved goodbye before magically transporting herself—and all her suitcases!—back to her home. Musa followed shortly after.

One by one, the other Winx fairies left, until only Bloom remained. With a sigh, she realized that she still had to pack.

"Ah! School break!" Bloom said happily. After throwing her stuff into two small suitcases, she left Alfea soon after her friends and traveled back to her hometown of Gardenia.

As she walked along the familiar tree-lined street toward her home, Bloom felt nervous. She wondered if her parents had gotten used to her being away. What if they liked having the house to themselves? What if they had turned her bedroom into a storage room? What if . . .

"Bloom!" Vanessa and Mike, Bloom's mom and dad, were waiting anxiously by the mailbox. When they saw their daughter, they ran to her and gave her an enormous hug.

"Thank goodness you're home!" Vanessa wiped away a tear. "We've missed you so much!"

"It's good to have you back, Bloom," said Mike. "Here, let me take your bags."

As Bloom and her parents went into their house, Bloom felt a huge surge of love for them. She couldn't tell who had missed whom more! As she climbed the steps to her bedroom and opened the door, she sighed with contentment. Nothing had changed—her room was just as she had left it. Her drawings still covered the walls, her clothes were still strewn around, and her bed had the same warm comforter on it.

Bloom spent a few minutes unpacking and then joined her parents downstairs. As she sat at the kitchen table, telling them about all the adventures she'd had during her first semester at Alfea College, she realized she didn't want to be anywhere else.

The next day was bright and sunny. Bloom woke up and brushed her teeth. She pulled on a colorful outfit and decided to ride her bicycle to Vanessa's workplace. Bloom's mom owned a small business called Vanessa's Flower Shop. During school vacations and summer break, Bloom helped out there. She hadn't always enjoyed the work, and she used to complain about it. Working had not been her idea of a good time, especially when she was supposed to be on vacation! But now, as she hopped onto her bicycle, Bloom could hardly wait to be with her mom.

Bloom pedaled breezily along the streets of her hometown. She felt on top of the world! Now that she knew who she really was—an actual fairy!—she was carefree and relaxed. Impulsively, she closed her eyes, spread her arms out like wings, and let the bike glide. She could do magic; she could fly! Nothing could hurt her.

Honk! The blare of a horn jolted her out of her reverie. *Whoa!* Bloom opened her eyes and grabbed the handlebars. She braked hard just as a fire truck pulled up beside her. Bloom looked up to see her dad, Mike, at the steering wheel. He was a firefighter, and Bloom had always thought that since he spent his days saving people, he was overly protective of her.

"Hey there, sunshine," he said.

"Hi, Daddy!"

"Heading for the shop?" he asked.

Bloom nodded.

"Make sure you keep your eyes open the rest of the way." Mike gave Bloom a stern look. "Just because you're a fairy doesn't mean you can't get run over."

Bloom ducked her head, embarrassed. "Sorry, Dad. I promise I'll be more careful."

"Good girl." Bloom's dad gave her a big smile. "See you at dinner," he said before driving off.

"Have a great day, Dad!" Bloom called after him. Taking a deep breath, she got back on her bike, making sure to keep her hands on the handlebars and her eyes wide open.

"Hi, darling!" Bloom's mother greeted her at the shop. "I'm just about to open the store. It's not as exciting as fairy classes, but would you like to help?"

"Of course I would, Mom!" Bloom gave her mother a warm hug. "I can't tell you how happy I am to be home. Fairy school is definitely exciting, but I'm so glad to be able to spend as much time as possible with you."

Together Bloom and her mother entered the small, cheerful shop. Bloom inhaled deeply. She realized how much she'd missed the smell of flowers and the bright colors inside the store. Happily, she set to work.

The store quickly filled with customers. As Bloom worked on arrangements and filled orders, her mom helped the walk-in customers.

Halfway through the morning, a woman came in looking for pink carnations.

"I'm so sorry, but I think I'm out of them, Mrs. Jeeves," Bloom's mom told her.

Bloom, standing behind a shelf filled with flowers and pots, spotted some red carnations. With a burst of inspiration, she touched them lightly, and presto! They turned pink. "Hey, Mom," Bloom called out, "we still have some pink ones here. . . ."

Mrs. Jeeves squealed with delight and walked off holding a lovely bouquet of pink carnations.

Bloom's mother was pleased, too. "It's nice having an assistant with a"—she paused, looking for the right phrase—"magic touch!"

Bloom and her mom exchanged a knowing smile.

Bloom's days in Gardenia went by quickly and happily. She'd never appreciated how much fun it was just doing ordinary things, like snacking on popcorn at the movies, having pizza nights, playing hide-and-seek in the park with Kiko, and describing her life at Alfea to her parents.

Then, right before she was supposed to go back to school, Bloom's world was turned upside down.

It started with a nightmare.

CHAPTER 4

Bloom had been asleep in her pink and purple room when suddenly she bolted upright, screaming at the top of her lungs, "Fire!" She was drenched in sweat and shaking all over, the most terrified she'd ever been. Her heart was racing a mile a minute. She could barely breathe. The Daphne dreams were nothing like this!

Her parents rushed into her room and flicked the light on.

"Bloom, what's the matter?" her mom asked worriedly.

"Did you have a bad dream?" her dad said. He went over and stroked her hair tenderly. "Don't be afraid. I've got you."

With those words—those innocent, reassuring words—Bloom's teeth started to chatter. The dream had been so real. *Too* real.

Bloom stared at her father. "I dreamed I saw you rescue a baby from a fire. And you said the same thing there: 'Don't be afraid. I've got you.' Who was that baby?"

Her mother looked stricken. "Oh, Bloom," she said as her eyes filled with tears.

Mike's face was ashen. "Try to go back to sleep," her father told her. "We'll talk in the morning."

Bloom tried to settle down into her bed, but despite her best efforts, she didn't get any sleep that night. She couldn't stop thinking about her dream. Who was that baby? And why was Bloom dreaming about her?

The next morning, the family sat around the breakfast table. Vanessa had prepared eggs, toast, and jam, but Bloom couldn't touch any of it. Her mouth felt dry and cracked. As they sat together, Mike kept clearing his throat but not saying anything. Bloom's mom was taking small bites of her toast, but she also seemed to be at a loss for words.

After a long silence, Bloom decided to speak up. "Mom, Dad, about the dream I had last night—it wasn't just a dream, was it?" She looked intently at both her parents. "It happened."

After a pause, Bloom's dad nodded miserably.

"It happened to me." The words slipped out before Bloom could stop them. It was an impossible statement—if she had been caught in a terrible fire as a baby and was rescued by her dad, she was sure her parents would have told her about it—but somehow Bloom knew it was true. Before giving her parents a chance to respond, Bloom said, "I need to know the truth. Tell me the truth."

Her parents exchanged uneasy glances. They looked as if they had to make one of the hardest, most important decisions of their lives right there, on the spot. Bloom felt a jolt of fear go through her. The truth couldn't be so bad . . . could it?

"Vanessa . . ." Mike's voice trailed off. Bloom had never seen her big, strong dad unsure of himself before. It shook her up.

"Yes, Mike." Bloom's mom was holding back tears. "I think it's time to tell her. She needs to know." Their faces heavy, Mike and Vanessa turned to their only child.

The hairs on the back of Bloom's neck stood up. Her stomach did a somersault. She jumped out of her chair and looked down at her parents. "Know . . . what?" It came out as a whisper.

"The truth, darling." Her father's eyes welled, and for a split second, Bloom wished she could take it back. Wished she hadn't said anything to make her father look so sad; wished she could forget about the nightmare. Wished she didn't need to know—anything.

"The baby you saw," Mike said, gulping, "was you."

Bloom had known the truth the moment she'd awakened from the nightmare. But hearing her father say it took her breath away. A lump formed in her throat, and her heart fluttered like the wings of a trapped bird.

Her father tightened his fists. "Sixteen years ago, I saved you from a fire."

Bloom pressed her palms on the table for support. "What was I doing in a fire?" she croaked.

"We have no idea!" her mother blurted out, upset. "Your father found you there."

"It was a miracle," Mike said thickly. "The building was completely engulfed in fire when my crew arrived at the scene. We didn't think there was a chance that anyone could be saved. But then when I was rushing through the building, I heard a baby's cry. I found you on the top floor. Everywhere around you, things were being burned to a crisp. But not you. The flames didn't come near you."

Suddenly, it all came back to her. In that instant, Bloom was mesmerized by the vision. She could almost feel the scorching heat of the flames licking the air around her. The fire roared in her ears, reflected in her eyes.

"It was as if the fire respected you. It . . . protected you." Mike spoke as if in a trance, still astounded by what he'd seen that day so long before. Gently, he confessed, "I don't know how you got in the building. You were all alone. But you weren't afraid."

Bloom's mom spoke up. "When Mike brought you home, he told me everything. Even though we had a hard time believing it, we knew there was something magical about you."

Bloom closed her eyes and took a deep breath. The words she tried to say got caught in her throat, and she had to fight to get them out. "But then . . . this means . . ." Bloom trembled. It was the hardest thing she'd ever had to say. "I'm not your real daughter."

"Bloom!" Her mom jumped up to embrace her, but Bloom backed away.

"You adopted me!" Bloom felt a surge of anger build inside her. "Why didn't you ever tell me?"

Her father looked sick. "We were going to, Bloom. We always planned to tell you the truth as soon as we thought you were old enough to understand."

That was lame, and her father obviously knew it. He ran his hands through his hair and shook his head in disbelief. "But then everything changed!" he said. "Fairies! Ogres! Magic schools! I mean, everything became so crazy, and then all of a sudden, we realized we were too late."

Bloom's mom gazed at her lovingly. "We never meant to deceive you, Bloom! You are the most important thing in our lives—you are everything to us!"

Bloom couldn't look her mother in the eye. She stared at the floor. Vanessa moved close to Bloom and tenderly cupped Bloom's face in her hands. "We loved you from the first moment we saw you." Her voice shook. "And we will never stop."

Bloom's eyes filled with tears, and she embraced her mother. Her dad joined them in a family hug. "No matter what, you will always be our daughter," he said.

"Yes, always," Bloom murmured. "I love you, Mom and Dad."

Bloom wasn't faking it. As she and her parents held each other, Bloom realized she did love her mom and dad with all her heart. The only parents she'd ever known, they were dedicated to her happiness and safety.

So what if they weren't her birth parents? They had always been there for her, encouraging her, supporting her. They hadn't wanted Bloom to go away to school, but they had allowed her to attend Alfea College because it was what she wanted . . . and needed. Their daughter's needs had always come before their own. If that wasn't unconditional love, what was? Bloom resolved to not let her parents' confession make a difference in how she felt about them.

But after that morning, Bloom couldn't help feeling that everything had changed. The rest of the week went by in a blur. She continued to ride her bike to her mom's flower shop and spend time with Kiko in the park. She still hugged and kissed her parents every night before bed. But all the joy had gone out of her school vacation. More often than not, Bloom found herself staring at the ceiling in her bedroom for hours on end, questions swirling through her head. If Vanessa and Mike weren't her real parents, then who *were* her biological mom and dad? Where did they come from? If she was a fairy, did that mean her birth parents were also fairies? Why did they leave her? Were they alive or dead? How in the world had she come to be in a burning building that would have collapsed if Mike hadn't rescued her? Bloom felt as if her past, which had seemed so normal, had suddenly crumbled before her. Now she felt like a stranger on Earth, with a secret history that she knew nothing about.

On the final night of school break, Bloom tossed and turned in her bed. She was glad she had been able to spend quality time with her parents, but she was anxious to return to Alfea. She needed a change of scenery, and she wanted to get back to her friends. And it would be a relief to start classes again so she could take her mind off the millions of thoughts and questions she'd been obsessing over.

The next morning, Bloom awoke early and packed her bags. She gave her parents a big hug before she left.

"Bye, darling. Remember, any time you feel like talking, give us a call." Bloom's mom held back her tears as she gazed at her daughter.

"We'll miss you, sweetheart," Bloom's dad said gently.

Bloom nodded. "Love you, Mom and Dad," she said. She took a deep breath, and with a wave of her hand, she transported herself back to the Magic Dimension, where her fairy friends awaited.

When Bloom arrived in the suite she shared with her friends, all the fairies were in high spirits. They were trading giggle-filled stories of their trips home and all the magical things they had done. Everyone seemed happy—everyone but Bloom. She tried to put on a smile, but she just couldn't do it. When Stella asked her how her vacation had been, Bloom excused herself and went into her bedroom. With a heavy heart, she curled up in her bed, squeezing her eyes tight to avoid the tears from spilling out in a river.

Finding out she was a fairy had rocked her world.

Finding out she was adopted had crushed it.

Memories of her life with Mike and Vanessa repeated in her head—there had been so much joy! Bloom remembered a lot—she even had a mental snapshot of her mom and dad cooing over her in the crib. She saw herself blowing out candles on every birthday cake through the years, opening presents on Christmas mornings, getting Kiko, ice-skating for the first time (and promptly falling on her behind!), plus all those summers at the beach . . .

She'd thought she had the perfect family.

Had it all been a lie?

As she burrowed beneath the covers, Bloom heard her fairy friends enter her room.

"C'mon, sleepyhead, get up! You haven't even seen all the clothes I got while I was at home!" Stella had failed to notice that Bloom was in no mood to see her latest wardrobe.

"Bloom, what's wrong?" Musa was the most sensitive in the group, and immediately could tell that something was up.

"Yeah, Bloom, you've hardly said a word since you got back. What happened while you were home?" Flora's voice was full of concern.

Bloom poked her head out from the covers. Stella, Musa, Flora, and Tecna were standing over her bed. As she looked at her friends, Bloom realized she had to tell them the truth. "Guys, I just found out a terrible secret from my past," she blurted out.

Tecna—the practical fairy—said, "Well, tell us about it, and maybe we can help."

The Winx settled into Bloom's room as she told her story. Musa and Tecna sat cross-legged on the floor. Stella perched royally on the end of Bloom's bed, filing her nails. Nurturing Flora leaned over Bloom, stroking her hair soothingly.

"Don't be sad, Bloom," said Musa when Bloom was finished.

"I know it must be a shock," said Flora, "but remember: your parents *chose* you."

"They love you," Tecna said matter-of-factly.

"So in a way," Musa said, "nothing has really changed."

"I know," Bloom said with a sigh. "But now I have so many questions."

Stella stopped filing her nails and peered over her shoulder at Bloom. "Questions? About what?"

About—everything! Bloom wanted to scream. Instead she got up and paced the small room. Maybe if she shared her feelings with her friends, things would make more sense. "I am a fairy," she said. "So how did I end up on good old nonmagical Earth? Who are my birth parents? Did I get my powers from them?"

"Yes, those are a lot of questions," Tecna said.

Kiko hopped onto the bed and nodded vigorously, for he, too, understood Bloom's dilemma.

Flora was thoughtful. "Are you sure you want to find the answers?"

"I have to know who I am," Bloom declared. She turned to her friends. "Winx, will you help me?"

No one hesitated.

"Of course!" promised Flora

"Absolutely!" vowed Stella.

"I'm right here," declared Tecna.

"You have our word," pledged Musa.

In a show of solidarity, the girls reached out and piled their hands one atop another and chorused, "Word of . . . Winx!"

Chapter 5

The next day, Bloom knocked on the door of Miss Faragonda's office. She had received a note from the headmistress asking her to drop by. "May I come in?" she asked. The headmistress was staring out the window, her back to Bloom.

"Oh, yes, Bloom." Miss Faragonda turned around and sat at her desk. "I'm glad you came. I wanted to see you."

Bloom tensed as she slid into the chair opposite the headmistress. They hadn't spoken since that strange day at the library. Bloom didn't know why she'd been summoned now.

Faragonda wasted no time. "I've been thinking about what happened in the library before school break," she said carefully. She leaned on her elbows and clasped her fingers together. "I know the one you are searching for is Daphne—"

"Daphne—yes!" In the middle of her family drama, Bloom had forgotten all about Daphne. But as soon as Miss Faragonda mentioned her name, all the dreams and nightmares came back to her. Bloom hoped that Miss Faragonda would tell her more about the nymph fairy. At the very least, it would be great to clear up one mystery in her life. Bloom was in luck, at least somewhat.

"Daphne was one of the ancient Nymphs of Magix," the white-haired headmistress said. "After much thought, I have decided to show you what I know about her. Come!" Miss Faragonda closed her eyes, waved her fingers, and cast a spell.

Show you, Bloom thought. Not *tell* you. That must mean . . .

Faragonda's spell took effect, and in a flash, Bloom was transported. She was no longer in Miss Faragonda's office, or anywhere in Alfea—or even above the ground.

Bloom and the school's headmistress were underwater! Water bubbled, cool and clear, all around them. Strange and fascinating fish and other aquatic creatures were everywhere.

"Wow!" Bloom was astonished. She could breathe underwater! And she should have been totally drenched, but she wasn't even wet. She didn't have to swim; instead she made footprints in the mud as she walked on the bottom of the lake.

"Daphne lived here," Miss Faragonda explained, as if this were the most natural thing in the world. "In the depths of Lightrock Lake. Come."

Bloom hesitated. Her nerves took over, and she froze. Did she really want to go farther? After what she'd just been through in Gardenia, maybe learning the truth wasn't such a great thing after all.

"It's okay, Bloom. Don't be afraid," the headmistress reassured her.

Together they tromped through the muddy bottom of the lake. After a while, they came to a cavern formed out of ancient boulders. From somewhere deep inside the cavern was a glow—like a flashlight at the end of a tunnel. Bloom was drawn to it. The light got brighter and brighter as she moved toward it.

Then Daphne appeared.

The nymph, her eyes hidden behind that orange and gold mask, was close enough for Bloom to touch. Bloom reached out and realized Daphne was offering something to her. It was a small chest, like a treasure chest, pink and gold and encrusted with gemstones. The nymph lifted the lid and placed it in Bloom's hands. Inside, a beautiful crown, something a princess would wear, glittered.

Bloom blinked. And—*snap!* She was back in Miss Faragonda's office!

The headmistress gasped and wiped her brow.

Bloom was speechless. "I . . . uh . . ." was all she could manage to say.

Miss Faragonda pulled herself together. "Bloom, I've shown you what I know about Daphne. I hope it is enough."

Enough? That was barely a start! Bloom couldn't begin to comprehend what she had just seen. How had she survived being underwater without air? Why hadn't Daphne spoken to her? Why had the dream nymph given her the treasure chest? And—Bloom looked around—where was it? The chest and crown had not come back to Alfea with her. "B-but I . . . ," she stammered, "I want to know more."

Miss Faragonda nodded. "I understand. But I fear what you are doing may be dangerous. You must end your search now." Without another word, the headmistress escorted Bloom out of her office.

CHAPTER
6

Cloudtower, the school for teen witches, was a dark, sinister castle with dark purple walls and dome roofs with a spike on top of each. The castle stood on top of a craggy mountain, surrounded by menacing storm clouds that gathered at the school every day.

That evening, the Trix sat at a table in the school cafeteria. They were on the upper level, which allowed them to look down upon the other diners. As they ate, they discussed events that had happened a few months before.

The Trix had discovered a powerful source of energy within Alfea. They had sneaked into the fairy college with a magic vacuum that could suck up and trap energy . . . but discovered that the source of power wasn't some*thing*, but some*one*. That someone had been Bloom. The Trix had tried to take Bloom's magical energy away, but she had defeated them singlehandedly and blasted them back to Cloudtower. Now the Trix were discussing their next move.

"We can't stop now!" Stormy hissed. She was the witch with wild, frizzy purple hair whose special power was creating weather disasters.

Darcy agreed. "Bloom is the most powerful fairy in the Magic Dimension!"

Icy, the leader of the trio, was thoughtful. Toying with her silverware, she mused, "I know, sisters, but we need to proceed carefully. We can't just destroy her—that would be wasteful."

As the Trix talked, a pair of witches at a table just below them overheard their conversation. One of them, a freckled girl named Mirta, called up to Icy, "Why are you always plotting to destroy them? Fairies aren't all that bad."

Icy looked down her nose at Mirta. "I'm sorry. Were you actually speaking to *me*?"

Mirta stuttered, "I—I only meant to say I think that maybe . . . we should try to get along."

Stormy exploded with laughter and then sneered, "Oh, how very Mirta!" The entire cafeteria joined in mocking Mirta.

"Mirta, let's go." Lucy, Mirta's roommate and companion, stood up abruptly and threw her napkin on the table. "I can't stand this anymore."

Mirta followed Lucy to their dorm room. Once they were inside, Lucy turned on her. "Why do you say those crazy things?"

"But Lucy . . . ," Mirta began. She didn't know how to defend herself.

"The whole of Cloudtower was laughing at you. It was so embarrassing!" Lucy said.

"It's the Trix!" Mirta cried. "They're so mean!"

Lucy's dark hair fell into her long, thin face. She declared, "I like the Trix. I want to be just like them. And not like you!"

Frustrated and upset, Mirta stormed out. The young witch headed up to Cloudtower's roof, where she could be alone to think.

"Those terrible Trix," she muttered. "They're making Lucy just like them. I've got to do something. Lucy and I have been friends forever. I won't let the Trix ruin it! I've got powers, too!"

Mirta's magic wasn't as easy to see as that of the other witches, but it was every bit as powerful—especially when she was angry. Like at that moment.

The harsh wind blew her hair every which way, but when she conjured up a glowing ball of light and chanted a spell over it, Mirta had a clear view of her target—the Trix. She could hear every word they said.

Icy had come up with a plan and was sharing it with Stormy and Darcy. "Sisters, we're going to trick Bloom. We'll make her think she's really a witch—not a fairy! This way she'll think she's a danger to her friends and run away. Once she's alone, we'll rip her power right out of her!"

"Oh, no!" Mirta exclaimed. "This is terrible! I've

got to find that girl. The Trix have turned Lucy against me, but I'll repay them in kind. I'll warn Bloom and expose them as the liars they are!"

Chapter 7

The next day, Bloom arranged to meet Prince Sky at an ice cream parlor in Magix City. She knew she wouldn't be good company, but she really liked Sky and wanted to see him. As they sat together in a booth, Bloom tried to be cheerful, but inside she felt gloomier than ever. She was still reeling from the revelation of her adoption, and was completely distracted.

At first, Sky didn't seem to notice. The blue-eyed blond Specialist was in high spirits. Over ice cream sundaes, he tried to entertain her with stories of his adventures. Bloom thought they must have been funny, since he laughed a lot in the retelling.

Out of the corner of her eye, Bloom noticed a family at another table. The father had hoisted his son onto his knee while the mother spooned ice cream for both of them. They were all laughing. A stab of pain shot through Bloom's heart. A week before, she would have thought the family was a lot like her own. They seemed so happy and normal.

"—so we tried it again and then we all fell, and we tried to get up, but—" Sky stopped in midsentence. "Bloom, you're not listening."

Bloom knew she should be attentive, but she couldn't help herself. She was trying to appear normal, as if everything was okay, but she wasn't pulling it off. She hadn't even touched her sundae.

Sky caught her staring at the table with a wistful glance. "What's the matter?" he said.

Should I tell him? Bloom debated. She gazed into his open, honest face. Sky and his Specialist friends had helped the Winx out of a few tight spots. They'd come to the rescue when ghouls besieged the fairies back in Gardenia. They'd helped them trick a monster in Alfea. Specialists were friends to fairies; they were natural enemies of witches.

Yes, I trust him, Bloom decided. Might as well come clean. But first she reached across the table and placed a hand over his. She owed him an apology.

"Sorry. I just need to tell you something."

Sky listened as Bloom described her nightmare. She told him she'd found out from her parents she'd been adopted, and told about the strange vision of Daphne that Headmistress Faragonda had allowed her to see. When she finished, Bloom looked at Sky, wondering if he would want to be friends after what he'd heard.

"Everything's changed," she said. "I don't even know who I am anymore. I have so many questions. . . ." Bloom trailed off hopelessly.

Sky tilted his head and rested his chin on his palms. "Well, let's see if we can find some answers," he said sincerely.

Sky's genuine concern touched her.

"You know I've been trying to find out about

Daphne," she said. "Who she is, how we're related—I mean, *if* we're related."

A trace of a frown crossed Sky's face. "And Miss Faragonda told you to stop looking."

Suddenly, Bloom had an idea. Her big blue eyes lit up and she raised her head hopefully. "If I can't use Alfea's library, I thought I could look—" She paused. Was this idea too crazy? No, she determined, it was definitely worth trying. "I thought I could look in the Magic Archive at Cloudtower."

Sky brushed his long hair back and whistled under his breath. "You want to break into Cloudtower?"

Bloom could tell from his expression that Sky was taking her seriously. She wasn't brave enough to ask outright, but would he—?

Sky reached out to her. "I'll help you."

Whew! Bloom let out a long breath. "It's kind of crazy," she admitted, grateful for his offer.

"Hey, what are friends for?" Sky shrugged one shoulder, trying to look cool. But Bloom could tell he was nervous.

♥ ♥ ♥

Bloom was right.

Sky attended the school for Specialists called Redfountain. Located in the Magic Dimension, it was next to both Alfea and Cloudtower. Sky roomed with his best buds, Timmy, Brandon, and Riven. After his trip into Magix City to see Bloom, he headed straight to see them. If he was really going to keep his promise to Bloom, he needed expert help.

He found Timmy sitting cross-legged on the floor of his room. Brandon lay on the bed reading a book. Taking a deep breath, Sky told his friends about Bloom's situation and her request to break into Cloudtower. Once he finished, there was a long silence. "So . . . will you guys help?" Sky asked.

Timmy wasn't judgmental. He focused on the facts. "The Magic Archive is one of the biggest collections of magical books in the Magic Dimension," he informed Sky. After typing away on his computer, he pulled up a detailed map of Cloudtower, complete with a diagram of the Magic Archive.

"Thanks, Timmy," Sky said. He scanned the drawing and frowned. "Bloom's determined to do this. So what do we look for?"

"Well, there's a book that will answer any question—you just have to ask," Timmy said.

"That sounds right—" Sky began.

Brandon cut Sky off. "Breaking into Cloudtower is completely crazy!" The brown-eyed boy had bounced off the bed and stepped up to Sky. Brandon was a really cool guy who tended to play it safe and stick to the rules.

Sky was a little annoyed. He didn't need Brandon's negativity right now. He placed his hand on Brandon's shoulder and explained, "Listen, Brandon. I told Bloom I'd help her, and I will."

Brandon folded his arms across his chest. "Whatever. Just don't say I didn't warn you."

Timmy was still thinking, studying the map. "I can show you how to find that book."

Outside Timmy's room, a fourth Specialist was eavesdropping on the boys' conversation.

"Well, well," Riven said, "I know someone who will be pleased to find out about this."

He turned away and strode down the hallway. Using his power of telepathy, Riven summoned his new friend. *"Darcy?"* he called.

"Riven! I hear you," the calculating witch answered.

"I've got something for you," Riven said.

"Oh, goody!" Darcy declared, rubbing her palms together in anticipation.

A trio of witches
called the Trix
goes to school
at Cloudtower.
These evil girls are
named Darcy, Icy,
and Stormy.

Darcy is an expert at using her powers of dark magic. She is able to hypnotize her opponents to confuse and control them.

Stormy conjures up violent forces of nature, such as tornadoes and lightning bolts, to do her bidding.

Icy, the oldest and the leader of the Trix, uses her ice-cold abilities to freeze enemies in their tracks.

Bloom is a powerful fairy with a mysterious past. Will she discover her true identity before it's too late?

Stella, the Fairy of the Shining Sun, is the first to tell Bloom that she has magical powers. Stella encourages Bloom to attend Alfea College, a school for fairies.

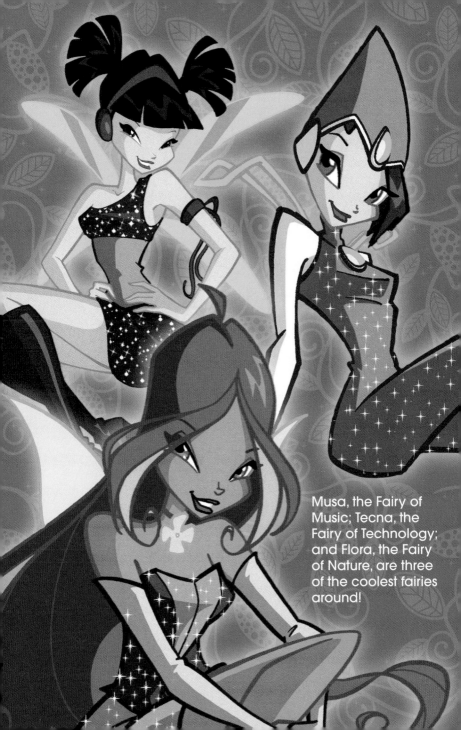

Musa, the Fairy of Music; Tecna, the Fairy of Technology; and Flora, the Fairy of Nature, are three of the coolest fairies around!

At Alfea College, Bloom and Stella become friends with Tecna, Musa, and Flora. Together they are the fabulous Winx Club!

CHAPTER 8

In the night sky, Bloom's long, wavy red hair blew in the wind. She was riding on the back of Sky's airborne motorcycle, her arms wrapped around his waist. They grazed the tops of pine trees and then skimmed the surface of a beautiful lake. The water gleamed in the moonlight.

"Almost there, Bloom," Sky called over his shoulder.

Sky had kept his promise. He was taking her to Cloudtower, to the Magic Archive. Bloom had pinned all her hopes on this one book. She believed it existed and would finally reveal the truth—about Daphne, and about Bloom's true identity. She was lucky to have a friend like Sky to help her. Between him and the Winx, Bloom felt she might just be okay.

Breaching the walls of Cloudtower was not a problem for an advanced Specialist like Sky. His powers enabled him to magically transport himself—and anyone with him—through walls, gates, bricks, glass, and barriers of any kind.

Once inside the witches' school, Sky led Bloom down a steep staircase.

Bloom's heart was racing, but she tried to keep it together. "So Timmy says there's one book in particular that we should try to find?"

"Yup," said Sky, consulting the digital map on his handheld computer. "And it looks like we're headed in the right direction."

"Thanks for coming with me, Sky," Bloom said as she trailed him down a long, deserted hallway.

Sky gave Bloom a tight smile. Suddenly, he came to a stop. The Magic Archive itself loomed in front of them. As if expecting them, the doors creaked open.

"This is nothing like Alfea's library!" whispered

Bloom. The air in the open space seemed to sparkle, while the darkest corners were shrouded in fog. Stacks of bookcases were jammed with books, scrolls, leather-bound volumes, and maps. Gilded statues of ancient witches and wizards dotted the place. A vintage globe was propped up on a pedestal.

It was after operating hours and the Magic Archive was empty, but Bloom could see that it had been used that day. Several books lay open, scattered on tables, book rests, and even on the floor.

Filled with anticipation, Bloom raced ahead of Sky. Then she felt his hand graze her arm and she stopped.

"Bloom, think about it," Sky said gently. "Are you sure you want to do this?"

No.

That was the real answer.

So far, uncovering secrets about her past had caused nothing but pain and confusion. But which was worse? Never knowing the truth about yourself, or finding out something you wished you hadn't? In the end, Bloom didn't think she could deal with so many questions that might forever go unanswered.

With a determination she didn't completely feel, she said, "I've got to find out who I am, Sky."

Only, the Magic Archive was so enormous, she had no idea where to start.

Sky took the lead. He began to page through a random oversized volume, musing, "Timmy said we'd know it when we see it."

He stopped. Out of the corner of his eye, he spotted something glowing. A lone book sat atop a book stand in the corner. As Sky and Bloom approached it, the book's pages fluttered as though touched by an invisible wind.

"I'd say this must be it!" In two strides, Sky was across the room.

Bloom's stomach was in knots. She stood back to let Sky check out the book first. Sky studied it, flipping through the pages. After a moment, he handed it to her.

"This is the book that will answer whatever questions you ask it," he confirmed.

Bloom stepped forward and took a deep breath. She was as ready as she'd ever be. She placed her palms on the book.

"I want to know," she announced in a clear, full voice, "who I really am."

Once the words were out, it was too late to take them back.

The vision that appeared in Bloom's head was straight out of a nightmare. All around was pitch darkness. Three black-clad masked figures flew right at Bloom. They had long, stringy hair and hooked noses. They were ancient witches, as scary a sight as Bloom had ever seen. What they had to say was the most terrifying of all. Pointing at her with long, crooked fingers, they cackled, "You are like us, Bloom. You are . . . a witch!"

Bloom's legs turned to jelly. She was horrified! How could this be? She shook her head to get rid of the image, but the ancient witches stayed. Their coal-black eyes bored into her.

No! Frantically, Bloom willed her mind to banish the witches, to make what they were saying not true. But there they were, still cackling at her. They'd come from the book, the magic book with all the answers . . . so . . . it had to be true, right? Finally, the vision of the cackling old crones faded away.

Bloom's large eyes filled with tears as she turned to face her friend. "Oh, Sky!" She could barely speak.

Worried, Sky came close. "What is it? What did you see, Bloom?"

"I saw three ancient witches, and they told me . . ." Sky reached for her. He was just about to close his hand over hers when Bloom blurted out, ". . . that I'm like them! That I'm a witch!"

Sky gasped. He withdrew his hand and backed away from the distraught girl. "You're a witch?" he gulped. "Oh, no!" Sky couldn't believe it. He was so sure he knew her, so sure he really liked her. But how could the magical book with all the answers be wrong? He stared at her, not wanting to believe what she was saying.

Pleading, Bloom reached out to him. This was the worst day of her life. She needed a true friend more than ever. She couldn't lose Sky. She looked into his eyes, but all she saw was fear. "Sky," she begged, "does it make that much difference to you?"

Sky's head was bowed. He couldn't even look at her.

Bloom's hand flew to her mouth.

"Sky?" she whispered. *Please don't hate me. Please don't desert me.* That was what she wanted to say. But already she knew it was useless. Nothing she could say or do was going to change Sky's feelings. He hated witches. All witches. Even her.

Say something! Bloom silently begged Sky. He didn't. He took a tentative step toward her, but he had hesitated a minute too long.

Bloom said, "Now I know. I finally know who I am. I'm a witch."

"I'll take you to Alfea," Sky offered, after a beat.

"No. I want to be alone. Please go." Bloom turned her back to Sky and collapsed into a heap. After a moment, she heard the sound of Sky's footsteps fading away. Bloom put her head in her hands and began to cry.

CHAPTER
9

When Stella woke up the next morning, she was surprised to find a fretful Flora knocking on her door.

"Am I late for classes?" Stella asked sleepily.

"That's not why I'm here," Flora said, coming into Stella's room and settling on her bed. "Bloom never came home last night!"

Stella's eyes widened in surprise. "Really?"

At that moment, Musa and Tecna burst in.

"We looked high and low," Tecna reported. "We checked the library, all the classrooms, basically the entire campus. Bloom is nowhere to be found!"

"We have to find her," Musa declared.

"I'll be ready in five minutes," Stella promised.

She dressed quickly and met the Winx outside the gates of Alfea.

The fairies started looking for Bloom together. Since they knew Bloom wasn't in Alfea, they went outside the college and stood looking out onto rolling hills, grassy fields, dense forests, and placid lakes. Bloom could be anywhere.

"The only way to find her is to use our powers," Flora said.

In unison, the girls chanted, "Magic Winx! Charmix!" And one by one, they summoned their special powers.

"Stella! Fairy of the Shining Sun!"

"Flora! Fairy of Nature!"

"Musa! Fairy of Music!"

"Tecna! Fairy of Technology!"

As they called out, they leapt high into the air. Delicate wings sprouted on each girl's back, and rings of light illuminated them, making their outfits sparkle. As soon as the transformation was complete, Stella called for action. "Winx! Let's get to it! Which way did she go?"

Flora used her magic and saw a vision of Bloom walking through a field. "Bloom was here—right where we're standing."

"The grass?" Tecna asked.

That still didn't tell them which way Bloom had gone. Flora had a solution for that, too. "Super Pollen!" she shouted, raising her arms up to the heavens. A series of concentric circles formed in the ground. Then a giant glowing arrow popped up, winking on and off like a neon sign. "Look, everybody—Bloom went that way!" Flora exclaimed excitedly as the Winx headed off in the direction of the arrow.

"Now we need to pinpoint her location," Musa told her friends. "Ultrasonic Probe!" she called out, and sound waves radiated out into the atmosphere. "Scanning complete," she said when she was done.

Tecna was up next. "Commencing data analysis," she anounced. A holographic map materialized and hung in the air above them, processing the data that Musa had created with her sound waves.

"All right, got it!" Tecna said. "The radar probe detected a fairy life-form right here—in

Gloomywood." She pointed into a dark forest on the map.

"Great," exclaimed Stella, "which means I get to do my favorite thing—light the place up!" Delightedly, Stella launched herself upward. When she was high enough to clear the treetops, she spread her arms out. "Rising Sun!" Stella sang out, and all at once a blinding light radiated from the fairy and shone over the forest. It was so bright that Flora, Musa, and Tecna had to cover their eyes.

"You guys!" yelled Stella from up in the air. "Now that I've brightened things up, let's go! Even with my powers, we don't have all day."

One by one, the Winx took flight.

Several miles away, in the dark Gloomywood forest, morning dew settled over the thick foliage. Bloom awoke from her slumber covered with twigs, branches, and fallen leaves. Yawning, she sat up and rubbed her eyes.

The night before, she'd stayed at the Magic Archive for hours, trying to deal with the awful truth, that she wasn't a fairy after all: she was a witch. Maybe that was why she'd never found out what her special power was, the way her friends knew theirs.

Eventually, she'd decided to go back to Alfea but must have fallen asleep on the way. Now, realizing she was nowhere near the school, she stood up, brushed herself off, and resolved to find her way back.

She hadn't gone far when she heard a rustling in the leaves. Footsteps! Bloom squinted. There, beyond the clearing, someone was hiding behind a wide tree trunk.

"Hey!" Bloom bravely called out. "Who's hiding there?"

A girl around Bloom's age wearing a T-shirt with a picture of a pumpkin on it revealed herself.

"Who are you?" Bloom asked.

"Hi," the girl said shyly. "I'm Mirta."

"My name is Bloom."

"I know!" Mirta told her.

"You do?" This surprised Bloom, as she'd never seen this girl before.

"I've been looking for you," Mirta said. "There's something very important you need to know."

Bloom groaned. She hoped it wasn't more bad news. She had already been through so much!

"The Trix want to trick you!" Mirta said.

Neither Bloom nor Mirta knew it, but the Trix themselves were closing in on them at that very moment. Stormy stomped through the forest. She burned a path through the tangle of trunks, brushes, and branches with lightning bolts that leapt from her fingertips.

"Stop showing off, Stormy," Darcy reprimanded her. "If you keep on like that, you'll set the forest on fire."

"Sisters, we are here to find Bloom. Setting this place ablaze is not part of the program," Icy added.

"Sorry, Icy," Stormy said.

Gathering speed, the Trix headed deeper into the woods. their evil laughter filled the air as they closed in on the unsuspecting fairy.

CHAPTER 10

Deep in the woods, Mirta explained everything to Bloom. When she was in Cloudtower, she had overheard the Trix discussing how they were going to tinker with a book in the Magic Archive. They wanted to fool Bloom into believing she was a witch! Knowing that the Trix were up to no good, Mirta had been determined to find Bloom before the Trix could complete their evil plan.

"So I'm not a witch!" Bloom was so relieved, she wanted to hug Mirta. Then her anger at the Trix flared up. "They tricked me. Why would they be so cruel and hateful?"

Directly above Mirta and Bloom, the sound of cackling split the air. Mirta recognized the evil sound before she even looked up. She gasped. Her hand flew over her mouth, and she began to tremble in fear. Bloom looked skyward. Mirta had good reason to be scared.

Icy, Stormy, and Darcy hovered above them. "Hello, Bloom." Icy's greeting sent chills up Bloom's spine. "I see that you have company. The little witch who transforms emotions into images. You two make a really cute little couple . . . a couple of losers!" she sneered.

"You . . . you horrible Trix!" Bloom sputtered.

"You're mean!" Mirta accused them.

"Mean?" Icy smirked. "Try diabolical! You've interfered with my plans, Mirta. I don't like that." Icy unleashed her power. Jets of ice-cold water flew from her fingertips and surrounded Bloom and Mirta. Before they knew what was happening, the fairy and the witch were trapped inside a huge block of ice.

"Now," declared the leader of the Trix, "all we

have to do is destroy that beautiful ice sculpture and rip the power right out of Bloom's heart!"

Just as the Trix were about to send a blast of magic onto the trapped Bloom and Mirta, a booming voice cut through the woods. "Leave them alone!" It was Stella, who had arrived with the Winx in the nick of time. Thinking quickly, Stella conjured up a powerful ray of heat and quickly melted the ice, freeing Bloom and Mirta.

Furious, Stormy aimed her rage at the Winx. Using her magic, she stirred up a fierce wind. The wind separated into twin tornadoes, trapping the Winx between them. Stella, Musa, Flora, and Tecna huddled together. As they tried to evade the tornadoes, Darcy conjured up a powerful ring that dropped and tightened over the fairies.

Bloom could see her friends struggling. *"Noooooo!"* she screamed at the top of her lungs. She couldn't let her friends be destroyed. Bloom summoned up her energy and felt herself transforming into a fairy. She cried out, "Magic Winx! Charmix!"

Bloom's wings unfolded. With a cry of defiance, she hurled herself toward the trapped fairies, but facing two tornadoes was too much for her. The force of the terrible winds blocked her and sent her flying backward. She landed hard and crumpled onto the ground.

"Bloom!" Mirta shouted.

"Ha, ha, ha!" Icy laughed triumphantly. Darcy and Stormy joined in.

Mirta felt a terrible rage grow within her. She was tired of the Trix always getting their way. She was tired of their cruelty and their hate. She was tired of them giving all witches a bad name. Mirta decided that the terrible Trix would not get away with this—not as long she had her own powers. She channeled her anger and concentrated on the Trix. Mirta's magical ability allowed her to conjure terrifying illusions using her powerful emotions.

A gigantic monster appeared out of thin air. It was a hundred times bigger than the witches and had scaly green skin and sharp, ugly claws. Bright orange light shone from oval openings surrounding its head. It was a monster created by pure fury, and with a mighty swipe it reached for the witches.

"Argh!" Distracted, Darcy lost control of her magic. The tornadoes disappeared, and the magic ring surrounding Stella, Musa, Flora, and Tecna dissolved, setting the fairies free!

Icy, Darcy, and Stormy were outraged.

Unfortunately, Mirta wasn't a very powerful witch. Her anger weakened once she'd set the Winx free. Her vision began to fade, and with it, her monster. It was gone all too soon—and just like that, the Trix gained the upper hand again.

"Not smart," Icy fumed. "This is it, Mirta! I've had it with you—you're a pain in the neck! You're a bothersome little . . ." Icy was so furious, she couldn't even find the right word.

Then she focused on Mirta's T-shirt and saw the picture on it. "Pumpkin?" She smiled evilly. "Why not?" She aimed a dark magic bolt at Mirta.

Trying to defend herself, Mirta covered her face with her arm.

It didn't work.

The Winx watched, stunned, as Mirta got smaller and smaller. Rounder and rounder. More and more orange. The poor girl had indeed been turned into a plump little pumpkin.

The Trix were thrilled! Victorious, the treacherous trio laughed hysterically, mocking the miniaturized Mirta.

"Ha, ha, ha!" Icy cackled.

"Ha, ha, ha!" Darcy echoed.

Stormy joined in, too.

But then Icy's laughter stopped in her throat. Her eyes widened in fear. Darcy and Stormy froze. All three witches looked up to the sky.

Hovering above them was Bloom. While the Trix were transforming Mirta into a pumpkin, Bloom had unleashed the full force of her fairy power. The entire forest was bathed in bright light, and for a second, all was white. Then, out of the light, the image of a dragon appeared in the sky. Its massive jaws opened wide and it roared! The force knocked everyone to the ground.

As quickly as they had come, the light faded and the dragon disappeared.

The Trix had disappeared, too.

"What happened?" Dazed, Stella got up from the ground unsteadily.

Musa scanned the scorched earth. "Where's Bloom?"

"She's gone!" Tecna exclaimed.

"Not again," moaned Stella.

"Yoo-hoo, I'm over here!" Bloom called to her friends. She had been thrown several feet away.

"Bloom!" The Winx, astonished but relieved, ran over to her.

"You really took care of the Trix." Tecna gave Bloom a big hug.

"I guess so," Bloom agreed. "But look what they did to Mirta."

The poor girl was still a little orange gourd.

Flora frowned. "Icy's spell was black magic, but I will try to help her. Let's get her back to Alfea."

CHAPTER 11

After returning to Alfea, Bloom should have been in high spirits. Her fairy identity was real. Using her fierce powers, she'd defeated the terrible Trix. But instead of feeling elated, she felt a horrible sense of loss.

Hunched over her homework, she complained to Kiko, "I can't focus at all. I keep thinking about Sky and what happened at Cloudtower. He hasn't called me since."

Bloom's ever-helpful pet rabbit had an idea. He mimed dialing the phone.

"Me? You think I should call him?" Bloom considered it. Was it possible that Sky was waiting for her to make the first move? She did have a lot of explaining to do. She decided to make the call.

It went straight to voice mail.

"What's the point?" Bloom moaned, deflated. "He thinks I'm a witch. No wonder he isn't calling, or answering the phone." Feeling foolish, she pointed an accusing finger at the bunny. "Kiko, you gave me bad advice."

The rabbit's ears flopped down.

There was a very good reason why Sky had not picked up Bloom's call. He was nowhere near his phone. He had left it in his dorm room at Redfountain while he trained for an important exhibition.

While Alfea was famous for its centuries-old castle, and Cloudtower was known and named for an imposing tower so high it reached into the clouds, Redfountain was made up of a walled-off fortress and boasted a gigantic arena. Many magical exhibitions had been held at the school for Specialists. One of them was happening the next day. It was an exhibition where Specialists had to not only demonstrate the various skills they'd learned in class, but also prove they could tame and control dragons.

Sky and his classmates had been practicing in the arena all day. Thousands of spectators had been invited to watch the students dazzle them with their amazing new powers. When Bloom called, Sky was in Redfountain's courtyard in the middle of sword-fighting practice with Riven. The boys held luminous transparent shields for protection. But every so often, a laser beam from the tip of a sword got through and nailed one of them.

"Yeah!" Sky exclaimed as he scored a point.

"I'll get you for that," Riven vowed ominously.

All over the arena, similar one-on-one battles were being waged. Wind Riders whizzed by as students raced their flying motorcycles through the air.

The students' headmaster observed them all. Mr. Saladin was silver-haired, a bit hunched over, and walked with the aid of a cane. Next to him, and twice his height, stood one of Redfountain's best instructors, Mr. Codatorta.

"All is going well, Codatorta," the headmaster remarked.

"It'll be a great show, Saladin," Mr. Codatorta boasted.

"I have high expectations for your Dragon Exhibition," Mr. Saladin said.

"My boys and I will astound everyone!" Mr. Codatorta was confident.

Mr. Saladin certainly hoped so. "Redfountain must show its advantage." He paused. "I've invited some very important people to this event."

Everyone at Redfountain knew the Dragon Exhibition was one of the most important magical events of the year. It put major pressure not only on Mr. Codatorta, but also on his students, including Brandon, Riven, Timmy, and Sky.

When Sky got back to his room that evening, the

first thing he did was return Bloom's call. "Sorry I haven't called you," he said, drying his wet hair with a towel. "I've been kind of busy training for the exhibition."

Bloom, thrilled to hear from him, couldn't stop trembling. It's a good thing he can't see me—I'm a nervous wreck! she thought. "Oh, that's okay," she said, trying to sound casual. "I just wanted to explain about the other night."

There was silence on the other end of the line. Bloom could feel her heart pounding so hard, it felt as if it would burst out of her chest. "I found out I'm *not* a witch," she said, rushing to get the truth out. "It was just a stupid trick by those three witches."

"Oh, well, that's a relief," said Sky, frowning. He hoped he sounded convincing. Even though Sky really cared about Bloom, thinking of her as a witch had made a certain detail of his life much easier. Now that he knew she was really and truly a fairy, things were more complicated. Sky was hiding a secret from Bloom—one he was sure would destroy her if she knew. Bloom's news was changing everything.

Bloom's voice came over the phone, interrupting Sky's thoughts. "Yeah, but it seems the Trix are out to get me, and I don't even know why." Bloom took a breath and spilled the real reason for her call. "Sky, I need to talk to you."

Sky's stomach twisted. His eyes fell on the holographic photo on his desk of a beautiful young girl. He didn't say anything.

"Can we meet up? Maybe at the exhibition?" Bloom suggested.

"The exhibition?" Sky repeated, stalling for time. What could he say?

"Yeah, what do you think?" Bloom's voice was filled with hope.

Sky shot her down. "Sorry, Bloom. It's only for VIPs. Got to go, bye!"

As soon as Sky ended the call, he rushed off to see Timmy. Trustworthy Timmy was the go-to guy when he needed a just-the-facts answer—without emotions getting in the way.

"Timmy, I'm in big trouble!" Sky told him.

"What do you mean?" Timmy, working at his desk, looked up.

"About Bloom," Sky confessed, "and Diaspro."

For a split second, Timmy looked at him blankly.

"Diaspro," Sky repeated. "The princess I'm supposed to marry one day. But the thing is, I really like Bloom."

Timmy scrunched his forehead. "Bloom? Well, I'm sure there's a solution to this. Let me think for a second."

Sky waited. And waited some more. It felt to him like a very long second.

Finally, Timmy said, "Diaspro is going to be at the exhibition, right?"

"So?" Sky didn't get the point right away.

"So give her the facts," said the logical boy.

"You want me to do what?" Sky was astonished at this advice.

"Tell her you have feelings for somebody else. Tell her you like Bloom."

Sky's eyes widened as he thought about Timmy's suggestion. It would mean some very angry royal parents and some bitter family fighting. He thought again about the picture of Diaspro on his desk. Eventually, he would have to choose between his royal duty as a prince and following his heart.

CHAPTER 12

Early the next morning, Stella, Flora, and Bloom marched into Musa and Tecna's room. Tecna was busy creating new scenic screensavers for her laptop. Musa was playing the flute, following sheet music around that floated in the air along with its music stand. Both flute and stand crashed to the floor when the three Winx barged in.

"Oh, Bloom, come on," said Stella, frustrated.

"Be reasonable." Flora, too, was trying to change Bloom's mind about something.

"What's going on?" asked Tecna, tearing herself away from her computer.

Stella flopped down on Musa's bed and crossed

her arms. "Bloom wants to go to the exhibition at Redfountain," she said, rolling her eyes.

Musa and Tecna were surprised. They all knew Redfountain was situated behind fortress walls and was not very easy to get into.

Intrigued, Musa asked, "Did she get an invitation?"

Flora shook her head. "She so did not! That's the problem!"

Bloom pouted. These objections were not welcome. She'd asked her friends—her best fairy friends—for support, and so far, she was getting none. "I need to go to that exhibition!" she told the other fairies.

"But Bloom, you can't," Musa said.

"That's what I said!" Flora reminded her.

"I need to talk to Sky, face to face." Bloom's determination was clear.

"Because—you like him?" Stella said teasingly.

"No, Stella, we're just friends," Bloom insisted stubbornly, but her face flushed with embarrassment.

"Well, in that case," Stella said with a shrug, "I don't see any reason to do anything crazy."

The Winx had boxed her in. Bloom had to admit she felt more than simple friendship for Sky. "I do like him," she confessed. "But I don't know what he thinks. I really need to talk to him." She paused. "Today!" she added, trying to explain the urgency of her feelings.

Flora folded first. "Okay, Bloom, I'll help you get in." The Fairy of Nature understood emotions best, especially when they involved matters of the heart.

Musa gave Bloom a quick hug. "It's obvious that Sky means a lot to you. I'll help out, too," the Fairy of Music said. Bloom gave her a grateful smile.

One by one, the other Winx fairies agreed to help. Huddling together, they hatched a plan to sneak Bloom into Redfountain.

Several hours later, Stella, Musa, Flora, Tecna, and Bloom appeared at Redfountain's back gate. The main gate was flooded with security, but around back, there was only one guard on duty. The girls chatted and giggled loudly to attract the guard's attention.

The guard wore a dark blue uniform and a permanent sneer on his face. Hands on his hips, he eyed them suspiciously.

"Hey, you! What are you girls doing here?" he demanded.

"We thought we would go see the dragons," Stella said in a singsong voice.

"Are you on the guest list?" the guard demanded.

The Winx giggled and shook their heads.

"Then scram!" the guard hollered, trying to usher them away from the back door.

With cries of laughter, Stella, Flora, Musa, Tecna, and Bloom put their plan into action. They scattered, running this way and that. No one person could chase after all five of them.

Or four.

While Stella, Musa, Flora, and Tecna distracted the stern security guard, Bloom had quietly opened the back door and snuck inside the fortress. She rounded a corner and breathed a sigh of relief. Score! She had done it! Now all she had to do was to find Sky. There were several hallways leading away from the back entrance, but it wasn't hard to figure out which led to the arena. All she had to do was blend in with the crowd of people headed down the corridor on the left.

But blending in turned out to be a bit of a problem. When Sky said the event was only for VIPs, he had not been exaggerating. The invited guests were a bedazzled bunch, decked out head to toe in lush royal robes. One tall, imposing man led the group. He wore a huge crown—was he a king? Many women were adorned with tiaras and sparkling jewelry. All carried an air of entitlement as they sashayed past Bloom.

In her faded jeans and boring T-shirt, Bloom wished she could skulk away. She'd never felt so insignificant in her life.

"Maybe this wasn't such a good idea," she said to herself, gulping.

Still.

She had made it past the gates. She was inside— and somewhere nearby was Sky. She knew she would be kicked out if anyone noticed her, but she had to try to find him. Bloom ducked down a different hallway.

To her surprise, all the way at the other end, was Sky.

Bloom smiled. What luck!

Or not.

Sky wasn't alone.

A beautiful platinum-blond girl bedecked in a regal white and gold robe had her arm hooked through Sky's. She wore a sparkling tiara, which meant she was a princess. Bloom felt something inside her turn cold and hollow. She ran around the corner to hide. When she peeked out, she could see Sky and the princess talking. Who's that? Bloom wondered, trying to stop a sinking feeling from overtaking her.

"I can't do this, Diaspro." Bloom could hear Sky's voice loud and clear.

"Sky, oh, Sky," said the girl Sky had called Diaspro. "Be serious." She gave a tinkling laugh.

"I am being serious." Sky was solemn. He seemed sad—and nervous.

Bloom needed to get nearer. She pressed her back against the wall and edged closer to them.

She wished she hadn't.

She watched, astonished, as Diaspro waved her

hands dismissively. "I know you don't mean what you're saying. You're my boyfriend."

Sky was Diaspro's boyfriend?

For a split second, Bloom could hear nothing—the blood pounding in her ears was too loud. Then it hit her—wait a minute! Sky wasn't that girl's boyfriend. It must be another Trix trick! Maybe they knew she was in Redfountain and had lured Sky and the princess together to make her jealous. "Those horrible witches," Bloom growled. "They're doing it to me again!"

Bloom raised her chin defiantly. This time, she would not be tricked. Silently, she followed the pair until it was time for Sky to enter the arena with the other students. As the exhibition began, Diaspro found a prime seat in the arena. Bloom slipped behind her, unnoticed.

CHAPTER 13

The exhibition was in full swing. Amid colorful pageantry and majestic music, the talented boys of Redfountain raced around the arena and performed amazing stunts on their Wind Riders. The stadium was full of well-heeled spectators cheering on their favorites, loudly applauding the amazing feats.

The Specialists were ace Wind Riders, and showing off their speed-demon motorcycle skills in front of a huge audience was exhilarating. As their capes flew in the wind behind them, the four boys raced around the arena in formation—Riven was in the lead, Sky second, then Brandon, and bringing up the rear was Timmy.

The audience oohed and aahed. The Specialists looked like the perfect team.

Until one of them broke rank—without telling the others.

While Riven was rounding a curve, he suddenly slammed on his brakes. To avoid smashing into him and causing a pileup, Sky, Brandon, and Timmy had to blindly veer sideways and hit their brakes hard.

Brandon and Timmy managed to stay on their motorcycles, but Sky crashed into a wall and bounced off his bike. Right away, Brandon left his Wind Rider and ran to his friend. "Are you hurt?" he asked worriedly.

"No, just a few bruises," Sky told Brandon, shaking off the injuries.

While Brandon was helping Sky to his feet, Riven, back on his Wind Rider, flew by them. This time he stopped short, purposely kicking up a cloud of dust in their faces.

"I've had it with you, Riven!" Brandon said, clenching his jaw.

"Whatever," Riven said, glaring at him.

Sky and Brandon, shoulder to shoulder, advanced on Riven, ready to take him down. They didn't even care that they were in the middle of the exhibition.

Timmy brought them to their senses. The realistic Specialist got between Riven and the pair, reminding them, "Guys—stop it. We've got to do the Dragon Exhibition!"

Timmy's timing couldn't have been better. The doors to the stables were just about to open. A collective gasp filled the air as four of the most amazing creatures in all the Magic Dimension cantered out.

They were tall, long-necked, graceful creatures, almost swanlike. But their bodies were wide, their wings mighty, their claws razor-sharp—and their jaws hid dangerously jagged teeth.

These fire-breathing creatures could do serious damage if provoked. It was up to Sky, Brandon, Timmy, and Riven to prove to the VIP crowd that Redfountain students could master these wild, mythical creatures. It was the most important part of the Exhibition, and the Specialists couldn't blow it.

The dragons trotted around the periphery of the arena. The Specialists stood dead center, ready to use their magic and skills. The Dragon Exhibition was about to begin.

From the arena, Bloom heard the crowd roar. She decided it was the perfect moment to confront this Diaspro girl, whoever she was. From her exalted perch, where she had the best view, Diaspro's eyes were on Sky. Bloom took a deep breath and confronted the girl.

"You're not going to trick me again!" she declared. She hoped her words would force the Trix to reveal themselves.

The girl turned and looked down her nose at Bloom. "What are you talking about?"

She would soon find out. Bloom bellowed, "Just like last time, I'll fight back! Bloom! Magic Winx! Charmix!"

She'd gotten better at summoning her powers. Within seconds, translucent wings sprouted from her backbone, and her whole body shimmered and sparkled. Leaping into the air, Bloom felt a surge of power. She had transformed into a fairy!

Diaspro wasn't afraid. She wasn't even impressed. If anything, she looked mostly annoyed. "I don't know what your problem is. But if it's a fight you want . . ."

Before Bloom realized what was happening, the girl called out a chant of her own. "Diaspro. Princex!" She glared at Bloom, removed a gold ring from her finger, and hurled it into the air. "You asked for it!"

The ring began to glow and widen. Before Bloom could get away, it encircled her and tightened. She was trapped inside the ring!

Bloom realized too late that Diaspro was a fairy and not another one of the Trix's nasty tricks. Not only that, Diaspro also had some pretty powerful magic at her command!

Bloom struggled to free herself, which was proving difficult but not impossible. With a mighty effort, she leapt high into the air and shimmied out of the ring's grasp. "I'll show you!" she challenged Diaspro.

But Diaspro was far from defeated. With a determined growl, she threw off her royal robe and soared upward—and headed right for Bloom.

It was on!

Meanwhile, the Specialists were in complete control of the Dragon Exhibition. Each boy, using a custom-designed remote control, was responsible for his own dragon. The creatures had bonded with their masters. Working together as a team, the pairs coordinated the show so it looked seamless. The dragons paraded around the arena, spread their wings and took flight, and breathed fire, all on command. The audience went wild. They'd never seen such an amazing display of the taming of these wild beasts.

About midway through the exhibition, Riven leaned over to Sky. "No hard feelings about the incident earlier, right?"

"None whatsoever," Sky assured Riven, but

inside he was seething. Riven had deliberately caused the motorcycle accident in front of hundreds of spectators, and had made the Specialists look like fools. Sky was determined that Riven wouldn't get away with it.

At last, his moment for revenge came. Riven was concentrating on his dragon and had stopped paying attention to the other Specialists. Sky reached into his cape and magically turned his remote control device into a huge boomerang. Before Riven could react, Sky swung the boomerang at an unsuspecting Riven.

Riven shielded his head with his arm—and lost his balance trying to avoid the boomerang. He went down hard.

So did his dragon!

Humiliated, Riven burned with rage. Blindly, he commanded his dragon to attack Sky's dragon. Riven's dragon hissed, and advanced toward Sky's dragon.

When he saw what was happening, Sky directed his fire-breathing creature to fight back. An unscheduled beast battle began!

As the dragons stamped their feet and fought, the audience was appalled! They'd come to see a family-friendly show, but instead were witnessing a brutal battle. Several people stood and exited the arena in a huff.

"Those fools!" Mr. Codatorta thundered. Livid, he raced into action to stop the Specialists' shocking shenanigans. He ran through the stands and heroically jumped onto Sky's dragon. "Back!" Codatorta shouted, trying to quell the chaos. "Get back!"

Dust stirred up by the dragons' feet flew everywhere. But the combat had spread past the mythical beasts to the Specialists themselves! Hand to hand, the Specialists started fighting one another.

Then it got worse.

A rumbling was heard through the arena that was not caused by the dragons. It led to an actual tremor: the entire stadium shook. The ground in the center of the arena split open. Smoke erupted from the crevice and filled the air.

The crowd coughed; their eyes stung.

The smoke lifted to reveal a new exhibition taking

place—another completely unscheduled and illegal event! Two airborne fairies were in the middle of a terrible fight. It was Bloom and Diaspro!

"So, have you had enough?" Bloom shouted at Diaspro, hurling a bolt of energy at the princess.

"No!" Diaspro volleyed back a lightning bolt of her own. "Have you?"

To the horror of the stunned onlookers, the two fairies looked as if they were trying to defeat one another—for good!

Diaspro screamed, "You're crazy!"

Bloom got in one last energy blast and hit her target straight on. Her rival keeled over and fell to the ground.

Sky was shocked. He bolted over to the fallen princess. "Diaspro—are you all right?"

"Oh, Sky!" Diaspro righted herself and rested her head on Sky's chest.

As she watched Sky comforting the beautiful princess, the truth hit Bloom like a sledgehammer. This was no trick perpetrated by the Trix. This was real. Sky really was with Diaspro. He had just never told her. Bloom thought her heart might break in two. To keep the tears at bay, she bit down hard on her lip. But it didn't help.

When Sky looked up, he was staring straight at Bloom's tear-streaked face. Sky didn't know what to do.

Diaspro did. "What is the matter with you?" she snapped at Bloom. Her piercing shriek could be heard throughout the arena. "This is the man I'm going to marry!"

Bloom's face fell. She wanted to die, right then, right there.

Sky couldn't bear to see her that way. Dropping Diaspro, he started toward Bloom. "Bloom, wait!" he called, reaching toward her.

But Sky was too late.

In a puff of magic, Bloom was gone.

Chapter 14

With a heavy heart, Bloom had transported herself back to her room at Alfea. She spent the afternoon buried under the covers of her bed, sobbing her heart out.

The next day, she learned just how much worse things had gotten after she'd left the arena. She found out from her friends that she was being blamed, along with Sky and Riven, for ruining Redfountain's entire exhibition. Headmistress Faragonda was fuming, and so were the headmasters of Redfountain and Cloudtower. The King of Magix had been in the audience and had left in a huff.

"Are you sure you're going to be okay?" asked Flora as the Winx prepared to go to class.

"I'll be all right. I just need some time to be alone," Bloom replied. After hearing about the huge mess she had caused, Bloom felt too ill to attend classes. Reluctantly, Stella, Flora, Musa, and Tecna left Bloom alone in the Winx suite.

A few hours later, Bloom found herself curled up with Kiko. "I made a compete fool of myself," Bloom told Kiko as she held her pet. The bunny looked on woefully. "And I did it in front of everybody in Magix!" It had been the most embarrassing moment of Bloom's entire life. She was so ashamed.

Even worse was the situation with Sky. "I thought maybe Sky . . . ," she said, sighing to Kiko. "But he's with that Diaspro." Deciding there was no way to save face, Bloom came to a decision. "I need to leave," she declared sadly.

She reached into her closet for her pink suitcase. Not so long before, she had packed it carefully, excited for her journey to Alfea. Now she tossed her stuff randomly into it, not bothering to fold anything or organize it in any way.

Kiko gave her a questioning look.

"I can't stay here," she explained mournfully. To comfort her, the bunny rested his head against her, and Bloom stroked his soft, fluffy fur.

She wanted to sneak out of Alfea without being seen. Her roommates would take pity on her, and she didn't think she could stand that. But in order to get out, she had to cross through the common area that linked their bedrooms. And of course, all four roommates were hanging out there. Stella and Flora were on the couch, reading. Tecna was pecking at her laptop. Musa was on the floor with her earbuds in.

There was only one way Bloom could get past them without being seen. She had to use her magic.

Spying Flora's magical potted plant in the corner of the room, Bloom cast a spell on it. The plant instantly expanded and grew to three times its size. Its petals opened and sprouted a seat wide enough for Bloom and her suitcase. She hoisted herself onto it.

"Come on up," Bloom told Kiko. Obediently, the rabbit popped into her arms.

No one noticed the giant plant and its passengers

traverse the room and transport Bloom out the door.

Once outside the gates of Alfea, Bloom boarded the bus to Magix City. She wanted to take one more stroll through the city before saying goodbye forever to the Magic Dimension.

The sun was setting on Magix City as Bloom walked the now-familiar streets. She passed by the fountain, peered down narrow alleys, and gazed up at the tall, majestic buildings. Memories rained down on her.

The day the Trix had trapped her inside a block of ice.

The first time her fairy powers had kicked in.

The day Stella had created a magical passageway and ferried her to safety.

Seeing Daphne's image carved onto the Hall of Nymphs building.

The carefree days of shopping, snacking, and chilling with the Winx.

The afternoon she and Sky had bonded over ice cream sundaes.

Bloom would cherish all her memories, always. But Sky had obviously moved on, and so must Bloom. "Goodbye, Magix." Bloom bade farewell to the Magic Dimension and started on her journey home. A lone tear rolled down her cheek.

No one had paid much attention to the sad girl with a suitcase and pet bunny—except for one particular shopper. Stormy happened to be looking through a shop window when she recognized Bloom. The purple-haired witch had exited the store quickly and followed her. Shocked by what she had heard, Stormy rushed to the café to deliver the news to the other Trix.

"Just like that," Stormy described, "Bloom said, 'Goodbye, Magix,' and disappeared!"

"She wimped out!" Icy was surprised, but shrewdly saw an opportunity. "How utterly perfect," she murmured.

Darcy understood. "I hear Gardenia is lovely this time of year," she said with a sneer.

When she arrived back in Gardenia, Bloom immediately went home and told her parents everything—about Sky, Diaspro, and her massive mess-up at the exhibition. "I can't go back," she said tearfully. Without saying a word, Bloom's mom and dad gave her a warm hug and held her tight.

Later the next day, Bloom's parents sat side by side on the sofa smiling at her. Bloom, curled up on the armchair opposite them, hoped they could help her untangle her mixed-up emotions.

Yesterday, going home had seemed like her only choice. Today, she wasn't so sure. Everything looked the same—Gardenia, the house, her room, her parents—but nothing felt right. She'd spent the morning doing her favorite thing, drawing. But every picture was of Alfea. Every girl, a fairy. Every boy, Sky. She tried to put her feelings into words.

"It's all right, Bloom, you don't need to explain

anything," her father reassured her. "You've made your choice, and we respect your decision."

In spite of her dad's vote of confidence, Bloom's stomach twisted into knots. "I hope I haven't disappointed you," she said.

Her mom approached and hugged her. "Oh, Bloom, as long as you are true to yourself, you will never disappoint us."

Bloom's eyes pooled with tears. "I love you, Mom and Dad." The old expression "Home is where the heart is" came to her.

Later, she lay on her bed, clutching a book about fairies to her chest. Staring at the ceiling, she thought about her friends—Stella and Flora, and Musa and Tecna. Bloom was born a fairy, so weren't the Winx her family, too? Wasn't Alfea also her home?

"Surprise!" Bloom heard a cold, all-too-familiar voice from the living room downstairs. The Trix! She sprang up and dashed down the staircase, her heart pumping wildly. When she reached the bottom step, she drew back in horror. Her worst fears were confirmed.

Icy, Darcy, and Stormy had invaded her house—and taken her parents hostage! Bloom's mom and dad hung suspended in the air, tied together with magic ropes.

The Trix had used their dark magic to conjure up a vortex in the middle of the living room floor. It was like spinning quicksand, threatening to pull everything into it that wasn't nailed down. Everything included Bloom's parents, whose legs dangled precariously over the whirling maelstrom.

Even though they were in grave danger, Mike and Vanessa's first thought was for their daughter's safety. "Bloom! Get out of here!" her dad warned.

A wave of terror washed over Bloom as she watched a houseplant get sucked into the whirlpool. Down it went—crashing through the basement, into the earth, into a black hole and certain destruction.

Bloom's parents were surely next. The only thing keeping them airborne was Icy's spell. If the evil witch broke her spell, her parents would plunge downward and get swallowed into the vortex. They would be gone forever.

Bloom had to act. She gripped the banister and faced the Trix. "Why are you doing this to us?" she demanded. "What do you want from me?"

"You really don't know, do you?" Stormy sounded amused.

"Leave my parents alone!" Bloom cried.

"Say goodbye, Bloom." Icy gave a hysterical giggle and then broke the spell that held Bloom's mother and father in the air.

Her parents screamed. They fought valiantly but uselessly against the ropes that bound them and the fierce power of the magical whirlpool. In seconds, they were sucked to their doom.

CHAPTER 15

"*Noooooo!*" Bloom wailed. She shrieked, "Bloom! Magic Winx! Charmix!" She transformed into a fairy—and immediately dove into the center of the vortex to rescue her parents. She had to get to them before they hit bottom.

Bloom willed herself to jet downward, faster and faster. Suddenly, she saw them! Her mom and dad were only a few feet from the black hole of infinity. They were plummeting fast. Bloom reached out to them. "Grab my hand! Grab my hand!" she pleaded.

But her parents couldn't hear her. Down, down they fell. Faster, faster Bloom raced. She didn't care about her own safety; all she could think about was saving her parents. But every time she thought she was close enough to reach them, they slipped away.

They were perilously close to disappearing. Bloom gave it one last try. With all her might and magic, with all her heart and soul, she blasted forward—stretching out her arms as far as she could. And then, a miracle! With the very tips of her fingers, she managed to get a grip on the magic bands imprisoning her parents. Bloom stopped their fall.

With her last ounce of strength, she flew upward, tugging hard, dragging her mom and dad back up to the surface. To their home, to the air, to their lives. Then she collapsed.

"Really? That's all you have? Stupid little Winx," Icy muttered, disgusted. She gave the other Trix the go-ahead to finish Bloom off. Darcy wasted no time. The witch struck out at Bloom. Stormy followed, tossing lightning bolts at the fallen fairy.

Bloom tried to defend herself, but the effort of rescuing her parents had left her too weak.

And the Trix knew it. "Give it up, Bloom! You're struggling in vain!" Icy said.

Bloom barely managed to raise her head off the ground. They had done everything they could to hurt her, and she still didn't know why. "What do you want?" she asked through gritted teeth.

"We're here for your power—the power of Dragon Flame!" Icy sounded diabolical.

The power of Dragon Flame? What was that? Bloom had never known what her precise power was. Apparently, the Trix knew—and they were there to rip it out of her. Icy explained why.

"Our ancestor witches found the source of the greatest power in the Magic Dimension. It was in you, Bloom." Icy sounded like she was accusing Bloom of something. She continued, "They had you. But that meddler, your insufferable sister, Daphne—"

"Daphne is my sister?" Bloom's jaw hung open.

"Daphne stole you away and brought you here—to Gardenia. So the ancient witches got rid of her. She deserved it, after all."

Bloom's head was spinning. Could Icy be telling the truth? Had witches killed Daphne?

"They destroyed Domino, your home planet, for good measure," Icy added.

Domino. A picture formed in Bloom's mind. She had been to a virtual Domino one day in class. It was a sad place. Dry, desolate—destroyed. Her assignment had been to make something grow there, to help bring it back to life. She would have, too, but the Trix had crashed in and ruined everything.

Icy glared at Bloom. "So now we're here to get what rightfully belongs to us—the Dragon Flame. And you can't stop us! Right, sisters?"

"Right!" they echoed.

"I can try," Bloom said with quiet determination.

"Oh, yeah?" Icy challenged. She threw a powerful bolt of ice magic straight at Bloom. It sent her flying backward and into a bookcase, where she hung suspended in midair, frozen solid. Darcy and Stormy laughed at her.

"You're the guardian fairy of the greatest power in the Magic Dimension." Icy moved toward Bloom. "But not anymore!"

Trapped, Bloom watched helplessly as Icy advanced, summoning Darcy and Stormy. "Ready, sisters?"

The treacherous trio banded together and began their evil ritual. They raised their arms skyward and chanted, "Vacuum!"

The Trix conjured up a triangular device that swirled in the air and pulled magic into it. It would extract the fairy energy from Bloom and deliver it to the Trix.

It was agony.

Nothing they had ever done to her before had hurt as much as this. Bloom felt as if her soul was being ripped out of her. As more and more of her fairy powers were leached away, the black-magic device shone more and more brightly.

After what felt like an eternity, it stopped. The swirling stilled, and the Vacuum disappeared.

"Sisters! I think we can go," Icy said, satisfied.

Bloom crashed to the floor, weeping. Every part of her body ached, but that wasn't why she couldn't stop crying. The Trix had taken everything from her. Without her energy, without her powers, how could she be a fairy? And if she was no longer a fairy, what was she?

To be continued . . .